THE YOUNG BLACK PRINCE

WRITTEN BY MELISSA MASON
ILLUSTRATED BY RYAN RAMOS

DEDICATED TO DANNY AND BRI

FOR YOUR YOUNG PRINCE OR PRINCESS.

This young black prince

Can climb a wall

This Young Black Prince

Can Stand So Tall

This Young Black Prince Can Build a Tower

This young black prince has boy power

This Young Black Prince Can Run and Hide

This Young black prince

Can go down a slide

This young black prince is bold and brave

This Young Black Prince is Pretending To Shave

This young black prince is ready for bed

This young black prince lays down his sleepy head

THE END

For more information on The Young Black Prince Series, please email me at melmasebooks@yahoo.com.

Follow me on the following links:

Facebook - @tybpseries

Instagram - @mel.mase

Twitter - @MelMase1

The paperback and eBook are both available to purchase on Amazon.

Printed in Great Britain
by Amazon